THE TEMPTATION OF WILFRED

MALACHEY

WILLIAM F. BUCKLEY, JR.

ILLUSTRATED BY JOHN GURNEY

ARIEL BOOKS

WORKMAN PUBLISHING, NEW YORK

Library of Congress Cataloging in Publication Data

Buckley, William F. (William Frank), 1925-
    The temptation of Wilfred Malachey.
    (Goblin tales)
    Summary: A poor boy in a rich boy's school,
Wilfred Malachey decides to help himself and his
friends by becoming a modern day Robin Hood, a
career that brings in a moderate income until he
discovers a genie in the school computer.
    [1. Conduct of life—Fiction. 2. Computers—
Fiction. 3. Schools—Fiction] I. Gurney, John, ill.
II. Title.   III. Series
PZ7.B882335Te 1985   [Fic]   85-40526
ISBN 0-89480-923-7

Workman Publishing Company
1 West 39th Street
New York, N.Y. 10018
Manufactured in the United States of America
First printing September 1985
        10   9   8   7   6   5   4   3   2   1

This book was set in Goudy Old Style and
composed by Accurate Typographers, Clearwater,
Florida. Printed and bound by R.R. Donnelley

Editor: Tom Durwood
Art direction: Armand Eisen
               Frazier Russell
Design: Barbara Bedick
Production: Wayne Kirn

WHEN WILFRED MALACHEY WAS SENT OFF TO BOARDING SCHOOL at Brookfield, he went by train. The Malacheys had been forced to sell the family automobile when his father's most recent manuscript was rejected. The publishers, Hatfield & Hatfield, had told him it wouldn't sell, because "Nobody wants to read about the Vietnam war." It had been four years since his father had sold a book. Six months before the fall term at Brookfield Academy began, the family had to move from Manhattan to a two-room apartment in Queens.

One night, Wilfred overheard his mother and father talking about Brookfield. His father said: "I don't care if I go into debt for the rest of my life, Will is going to Brookfield. Period!" When Wilfred's father spoke that way (sometimes he banged his fist on the table, but only after a couple of beers) there was nothing to be done about it, and Mrs. Malachey would simply shrug her shoulders and change the subject.

On the train, Wilfred's mother told him they could send him only five dollars every month. Wilfred said that five dollars wouldn't keep him in chewing gum.

"In that case, Wilfred, you're going to have to cut down on your chewing gum," his mother snapped.

Wilfred said — to himself: his mother did not take any lip from Wilfred — that he would find other ways to live the way the Brookfield boys lived. "If at Brookfield they're human," Wilfred muttered. "Which I doubt." He was feeling grouchy, and a little nervous, going to Brookfield for the first time.

THE BROOKFIELD COMMUNITY was aware that things had gone badly for the school during recent years. Everything went wrong that could go wrong: the pipes had burst in the main building; the large barn that housed the student activities center had burned almost to the ground (of course, the school was underinsured); the new tractor with which the vegetable gardens and the corn were tended during the summer had suddenly ceased to work, and by the time it was fixed the damage to the

gardens and fields was irreversible. "The place seems haunted," said Xavier Prum, Headmaster.

Brookfield was well north in Vermont, so that the winters came early, and Wilfred was happy at his first opportunity to learn ice-skating. One day, with some excitement after the first snowfall, he signed up on the bulletin board to ski. The athletic director, Mr. Kiphuth, handed an application form to Wilfred and asked him to sign a slip authorizing one hundred dollars to be charged to his parents.

Wilfred looked up. He lowered the pencil onto the table. "I think," he said to Mr. Kiphuth, "I'll just stick to skating." Mr. Kiphuth looked at Wilfred and said nothing. That night, at faculty tea, Mr. Kiphuth asked the Headmaster whether young Malachey's family was especially hard up. Xavier Prum answered, "If you ask me, Bob Malachey is flat broke. He's a has-been as a writer."

"How's he paying for Wilfred's tuition?"

"I'll tell you after he makes the payment for the rest of the semester. All I have from him" — and this was near to Thanksgiving — "is his deposit of last July. Either the remaining tuition comes in before Christmas, or Wilfred will have to do his

10

ice-skating in Queens. We just aren't in a position to extend charity."

Kiphuth said that was too bad. "A bright boy. George Eggleston tells me he's a whiz in computers."

"Well, maybe Malachey will invent a computer game and bail out his old man," the Headmaster said, picking up the *Brookfield Academy News* to read about last month's hockey victory over St. Paul's.

It was about then that Wilfred Malachey decided to take up seriously the matter of his personal poverty. He thought a great deal about it and carefully studied the habits of his fellow students, most of whom clearly were not worried about expenses. Josiah Regnery, for instance. Josiah received a monthly allowance of one hundred dollars from his father and often took two or three boys to the Creamery, the local drugstore, for ice cream sundaes.

Josiah was a chubby, good-natured boy who was easily distracted. When Mr. Eggleston was trying to teach him geometry, Josiah would simply stare into space. One afternoon, when the trees all around them were red and gold, he told Wilfred as they were skating that he was quite apprehensive about the math exam coming up at midterm. "To tell you the truth, Wilfred, I don't know the difference between an issasseles triangle and an equilateral triangle."

Wilfred smiled as he maneuvered the puck they were idling with along the ice. "What's so hard about remembering that an equilateral triangle is equal — get that, equi? equal? — on all three sides?"

"Okay," Josiah said. "But what about the issasselese triangle? What's that?"

Wilfred took Josiah's hockey stick from him and laid it out on the ice, positioning his own so that the handle touched Josiah's at an angle of about forty-five degrees. "There. Our two sticks are the same size, the two sides of an isosceles — that's i-s-o-s-c-e-l-e-s — triangle are the same size. What's so hard about that?"

"What's hard," said Josiah, "is to remember it all. All I can remember is that there'll be time after practice and before study hall to go to the Creamery for a butterscotch sundae. What do you say?"

"I'm broke right now."

"I'll pay. You teach me about triangles, you get one butterscotch sundae."

"You know," Josiah said as they sat in the little booth, the light snowfall breaking up the bright afternoon sun, "I think I could figure out a way for you to take my midterm exam. It's just *this* simple . . ."

Josiah had, in fact, figured it all out.

There were no fixed seating arrangements in the classrooms where exams were held at Brookfield. All that would be needed was for Wilfred to manage to sit down, casually, at a desk next to Josiah's. Wilfred, Josiah explained, would then write down the answers to each of the exam problems on a sheet of scratch paper. Then he would spill his scratch pad on the floor, having detached the top sheet from the pad before it was dropped. He would then simply bend over and pick up the scratch pad, leaving the detached sheet on the floor.

A moment later, Josiah would lean down, pick up the sheet with the answers on it and copy Wilfred's solutions in his own exam book.

"It's worth twenty dollars to me," Josiah said, intending to close the question.

Somewhat to his surprise — cheating was simply not one of the things the Malachey set thought it quite right to do — Wilfred hesitated. Cheating was one of the things one, well, one wasn't supposed to do. On the other hand, one was not supposed to be — how did his father put it? — "one's brother's keeper." He wrestled with the conflict, but eased toward the feeling that, after all, he wasn't personally responsible for other boys' behavior. "Okay," he said.

THAT NIGHT, LYING ON HIS BED after Lights Out, Wilfred chatted with his roommate, Steven Umanov. Steve was a quiet, studious, no-nonsense boy. His parents had come to America from Russia soon after the World War. Steve's father was a nuclear physicist who worked for the Defense Department. Steve took great

pride in this. He confessed to Wilfred that he, too, hoped to become a great scientist, "Like my dad." Wilfred was feeling argumentative and maybe a little disillusioned because he hadn't straightened out in his own mind the deal he had made with Josiah.

"How do you know your father is a great scientist?" Wilfred asked belligerently.

Steve hardly expected that claims about his father's prowess would be questioned. "How do *I* know it? I *know* it, that's all. Maybe one day your father will write a book about my father, assuming your father hasn't forgotten how to write books!"

All of Wilfred, which came to 120 pounds, sprang across the dark room onto Steven Umanov, whose body he pounded with clenched fists until the dorm master came barging in, swearing in that careful way peculiar to prep school masters (none of the serious stuff). *"Damn it, damn it I said!* I said damn it! What in the hell is going on, you . . . dumb . . . kids! Cut the damn business out . . . !"

Mr. McGiffert separated them. He told them he would place them both in the boxing ring the next day, so they could "get the resentments out of their system." "I hope you knock each other out," he added. Mr. McGiffert told them if he heard

one more sound from Room 28, he would lead them to the Headmaster. "You'll see what Mr. Prum has to say about this kind of . . . uncivilized . . . behavior. Maybe he'll take away your Thanksgiving privileges. Just don't say Mr. McGiffert didn't warn you."

Wilfred didn't sleep much that night. He bitterly resented Steve's crack about his old man. But he also figured the best way to protect his father was to act as though Robert Malachey, the well-known author, was engaged in a long-term research project and was taking very good financial care of his son. "Foreign royalties," he decided he would say, casually. Ah, all those books that Robert Malachey had written in the past twenty years, translated into all the usual languages . . . plus Swedish, and, er, Hindustani, and Japanese, and Australian. "The royalties," he would teach himself to say, "do mount up, you know."

Wilfred decided he would devote all his energies to doing something concrete about his disadvantages. He would become a — he toyed with the word — thief. Not a nice word. So instantly he stopped using it. Instead he thought of himself as Robin Hood, the great English woodsman. At Fire Island he had seen an old Robin Hood

14

movie with Errol Flynn. Flynn was unmistakably the hero of the movie, who would question that? Robin Hood took money from the fat rich in order to give it to the lean poor! True, in this case Wilfred would be taking from the rich to give to Wilfred; but since he himself was poor, that would not matter. And if there was money left over, he would give it to other poor boys — he knew that Tony Cobb had a hard time of it, also Red Evans. He would find ways to make life easier for them. The point now, having decided he was not really a thief, was to become a very clever thief — or rather, a very clever Robin Hood.

The important thing, of course, was not to get caught. If Errol Flynn had been caught, he would have been hanged. Hanged right there, in the public square at Nottingham. Led up the thirteen steps (thirteen steps? or was that the Tower of London, where they executed all those wives of Henry the VIII?), clump, clump, clump, up those steps, however many there were, then the executioner approaches you with a kind of ski hood, only it goes right over your eyes, and then — after you have a chance to say a prayer — BANG! The floor under your feet evaporates, and that is the end of Robin Hood.

Lying in his bed that night, Wilfred knew he would not be hanged if caught, but he knew it would be very unpleasant. His mother would be very disappointed, to say the least, and his father would never again talk about the Malacheys' tradition of going to Brookfield Academy.

And then, returning to the point at which he had begun his thinking that night, he turned his head toward where Steven Umanov was sleeping and said to himself:

"Steven Umanov, your father may be a great scientist. But he is also the father of a boy at Brookfield Academy who will soon be poorer than he is now."

Before the week was over, Wilfred had eased two dollars out of Steve's wallet.

"Two dollars. That way he won't notice," Wilfred said to himself. His confidence growing, he allowed himself a smile. For one thing, Errol Flynn always smiled. The greater the danger, the greater the smile.

AFTER THANKSGIVING, WILFRED was named Sunday Services collector, for the balance of the term, his jurisdiction being the left side of the Brookfield Chapel. The Headmaster had made it a point with the parents that the boys at Brookfield were expected to contribute to the Sunday collections ("even if it's only a nickel") so that they get used to the idea of giving *something*.

Wilfred's half of the church — one hundred boys, twenty or thirty faculty, staff and visiting parents — usually contributed in the neighborhood of sixty dollars. On a particular Sunday, that figure minus four dollars was what was turned in by Wilfred Malachey to the Matron in the sacristy.

Wilfred considered volunteering for regular duty, year-round, as a Sunday Services collector.

Around the same time, he began complaining of headaches to the Matron. There was talk, when the school doctor could find nothing wrong, of sending him to Rutland for a thorough examination; then always the headaches, after a troublesome day or so, would go away. The Matron was persuaded that they were caused by an allergy and nothing to worry about.

And so it was that during the afternoons, when the Matron excused him (because of his headaches) from regular athletic activity, Wilfred would make the rounds of the deserted dormitory rooms. He counted it an average day when he cleared between ten and fifteen dollars. His problem at the bursar's office was eased when his mother, just after Thanksgiving, sent in a check for the semester's tuition, Wilfred having no idea how his mother had got hold of two thousand dollars.

By February, Wilfred Malachey was skiing regularly. He had even qualified for the slalom competition at Stowe. Occasionally he would treat one or two of the boys to sundaes at the Creamery. He was frustrated by his inability to take math examinations more often for Josiah Regnery, who was now paying a hefty fifty bucks per exam. But he had not figured out a way to take more exams for Josiah than Josiah had to take. Cheating for more than one person was risky, really risky; and Wilfred was

determined not to take unnecessary risks. Unlike Robin Hood — who could go to the center of the town, with minimal disguise and only his bow and arrow and horse, and smite the enemy to the ground and ride triumphantly away — Wilfred had no horse, no bow or arrow, and no sanctuary. He had to be very, very careful.

IT HAD BEEN WIDELY NOTICED that when George Eggleston came back from the Christmas holidays, he was driving a new Mercedes 380SL. It was obvious to everyone that Mr. Eggleston could not possibly have purchased that car on the salary of a math teacher at Brookfield Academy.

George Eggleston had passed the word that an aunt he never really knew (hence his lighthearted attitude toward her) had "departed from this vale of tears," leaving him a little legacy. "I blew it all on this Mercedes," he said happily.

Two weeks later, the boys who were studying computers got the astonishing news that the Brookfield Academy would any day now have an IBM Mainframe Computer, an astonishing, luxury, state-of-the-art 4341, worth half a million dollars!

How had Brookfield been so fortunate?

George Eggleston explained at a faculty meeting that over the summer vacation he had been in conversation with a wealthy Brookfield alumnus who, learning about his ambitious computer instruction program, decided to make a donation. The donor had imposed a single condition, namely, the requirement of anonymity.

"Yes, yes, George," the Headmaster had said to Eggleston when they were alone in his office. "I know all about alumni and anonymity. But there is no such thing as anonymity from the Headmaster. So. Who gave us the IBM?"

George Eggleston, not in the least apologetic, said he had given his word and could not betray the identity of the benefactor.

"He will have to remain anonymous, Mr. Prum." (All the junior masters called the Headmaster "Mr. Prum.")

Mr. Prum let it go. Actually, he had no alternative.

WILFRED MALACHEY WOULD NOT HAVE KNOWN about this controversy in the administrative circles of Brookfield, except that Mr. Eggleston elected to chat with him about it, repeating (dramatically) the details. Wilfred had taken to staying in the computer hall after class, which went from eleven to twelve o'clock with lunch at a quarter to one. Wilfred stayed those extra forty-five minutes to watch Mr. Eggleston perform one after another of those seemingly magic feats the computer manuals were coaxing Wilfred to try. Before long, Wilfred had been catapulted way beyond what the manuals had intended.

During the Christmas holidays, Wilfred gave up a car trip to Disneyworld (his father was writing a travel piece for the *New York Times*) when Mr. Trevor, Frankie's father, passed on the word through his son that if Wilfred wanted to, he could spend his days at Mr. Trevor's office in the Chrysler Building. Mr. Trevor was a computer consultant, and in his office kept the latest models, to test them and to write manuals on how to operate them. Although Mr. Trevor was very enthusiastic about his work, he had never been able to interest Frankie. So when he discovered that Frankie's friend Wilfred was "a computer nut," the invitation had been tendered; for over two weeks, Wilfred lived with computers, putting them through their paces, making notes of what Mr. Trevor taught him.

By late February, Wilfred was in the habit of spending his non-classroom time (when he was not required by the athletic director to be at the hockey rink) in the computer hall, prepared to spend hours there exploring the latest challenges Mr. Eggleston had suggested to him.

Wilfred had long since been introduced to programming, first with BASIC, then with Pascal. Now his mind was crowded with possibilities. He wanted to press his knowledge of computer science as far and as fast as he could.

He had made up with Steven Umanov. Now, when Lights Out was sounded, he said goodnight to the dorm master at 10:15; then he stuffed a pillow under his bedsheets, put on pants and a sweater and, with the cooperation of Steven, who would cover for him if a proctor came around to check ("He's in the bathroom"), tiptoed out of the dorm. Setting his course through the shadows, outside the lights that illuminated the Brookfield Quadrangle and the great oak trees scattered about the main buildings, he would make his way to the computer hall, lodged in the tower of the Flagler Building, next to the astronomy lab. He was prepared to spend hours there as he had done earlier tonight. He had Mr. Eggleston's extra key to the hall, given to him a month earlier when Wilfred, after spending five consecutive hours on a project, managed to reverse an incredibly intricate program that Mr. Eggleston had mistakenly got himself locked into.

"You deserve this, Wilfred," Mr. Eggleston had said. "Use the computer whenever you want it."

Wilfred worked two hours and felt suddenly sleepy. He decided to nap rather than return to his room; he wanted to get on with the program he had so nearly completed.

He was excited about this, as he had taken up celestial navigation the summer before on Fire Island. Wilfred wondered whether he could program the computer to give him the name of any given star, provided that he entered the angle of that star, the exact time he spotted it and his estimated location within thirty miles. His father's last successful novel (ten years ago) had been about a husband and wife who were sailing the South Pacific when she fell overboard one night while he was off watch. The husband woke up and tried desperately to retrace the boat's path, but got mixed up because he didn't know which star was which.

The problem had stayed in Wilfred's mind, and Mr. Eggleston had suggested a formula by which the question might be attacked. Wilfred had sent away to the library at the University of Vermont for the Almanac and the Star Reduction Guide.

But right now he had to close his eyes. He walked the half-dozen steps from the computer desk to the old couch that rested at the corner of the room. After removing the pile of magazines and books, as several times he had done before, he stretched out and was soon asleep.

He woke suddenly. The door had creaked open. He heard the cold wind whistling outside. He looked at his watch; it was after two in the morning. Even Mr.

Eggleston, so informal and permissive, would be angered if he found him up at this hour, and might even suspend his privileges. He sat up noiselessly on the couch and reasoned that if he simply stayed quiet, in the dark corner on the couch, chances were that Mr. Eggleston would do whatever he intended to do at this odd hour and then leave, after which Wilfred could return, undetected, to his dormitory.

George Eggleston walked stealthily into the room, went up to the computer and snapped on the main switch.

He reached down to the bottom drawer on the left side and pulled it open. He took out a little aluminum box. From his pocket he took out a key and opened the box. He pulled out a notebook and an eight-inch floppy disk.

He inserted the disk into a drive in the mainframe.

The large screen leapt to life, and from his seat ten feet away Wilfred had no difficulty seeing what it was that George Eggleston was typing. He was carefully copying out a formula that appeared on the screen as he punched it in.

It was, of course, pure gibberish. Except that Wilfred knew that in computer language there is no such thing as gibberish. He knew that things like "ad4af5ag8pp/

could be used, as his father would say, "to make sense out of a *New York Times* editorial."

But why all the secrecy? Why the locked notebook, and the locked floppy disk?

After he had copied the long formula, George Eggleston brought his right index finger down on the RETURN key.

The screen seemed to go wild. It was filled with lines, then radials, then bright colors that grew gradually pale, and from the center a tiny white dot, the size of a pinhead, gradually increased in circumference to the size of a full moon that touched all four sides of the screen.

Slowly, the words appeared on the center of the screen:

"WHAT DO YOU WANT FROM THE OMEGAGOD?"

George Eggleston looked down quickly at his little notebook and copied out:

"You are the Omegagod and I am your faithful servant George Eggleston."

He then lifted his eyes from the notebook and wrote out:

"I want Marjorie Gifford to fall in love with me."

On the screen there was no action. It was as if the Omegagod were weighing Mr. Eggleston's request. Suddenly the capital letters began to appear:

"IT SHALL BE SO. BUT DO NOT CALL ME AGAIN FOR THIRTY DAYS."

Wilfred could hear Mr. Eggleston breathing deeply. He pushed the RETURN key. Then he withdrew the disk tenderly from the IBM's disk drive, replaced it in the aluminum box together with the little notebook and turned off the main computer. He walked back to the entrance of the room, switched off the light and was gone in the great swish of air that blew in as he opened and then closed the door.

Wilfred waited ten minutes before easing himself out the door. He looked carefully about for the wandering night watchman, then treaded softly but determinedly through the windstorm to the South Dorm. He dove into his bed and into a deep sleep, from which Steve Umanov needed to shake him vigorously the next day at Morning Bells.

He had dreamed it all, Wilfred thought. He came close to blurting out his dream, and its startling details, to Steven, but he thought better of it. What, after all, was the point?

MARJORIE GIFFORD CAME TO BROOKFIELD every Monday from Rutland to teach the boys who wanted training in piano. In addition, she taught a course in harmony to the three students interested in the structure of music.

She was hindered by the enthusiasm of a number of unmusical students who would suddenly announce to their parents that they wanted to learn piano. What they really wanted was to be in the company of Miss Gifford. She was twenty-four years old and petite, her hair styled in a simple pageboy. Her face was quietly beautiful, but it was the force of her personality that dazzled students and faculty alike — her humor, her solicitude, the profundity of her devotion to her work.

George Eggleston, the thirty-year-old, bookish scientist, had several times asked Majorie Gifford to dine with him after her classes. But always she would smile engagingly and tell him she had to get back on the early bus and study, during the hour's journey, a book that would help her work out an orchestration she was doing for the Vermont Symphony Orchestra. She gave the same excuse to the three other bachelors at Brookfield who tried so hard to engage her special attention. Week after week, month after month, she would simply smile and, after doing her teaching, be driven off to the bus station by the school superintendent, and for a day or so after she left, Brookfield would seem quite empty without her.

On the Monday after his episode in the computer hall, Wilfred made it a point to observe Marjorie Gifford. At lunch at Commons, she sat next to Mr. Eggleston. She had to sit next to *somebody*, Wilfred told himself. It had to be coincidence. That evening, at six as usual, Miss Gifford left the school; but instead of getting into the station wagon to go to the bus station, she drove away from Brookfield with Mr. Eggleston in his Mercedes-Benz.

Three weeks later, Miss Gifford was seated at the piano in the assembly hall. After the hymn, after the morning scriptural reading, after the routine daily announcements, the Headmaster broke out in what Josiah Regnery called "the Headmaster's inscrutable smile" (usually it came before a half-holiday was announced for that afternoon).

"I have some very happy news for the boys of Brookfield, indeed for the whole Brookfield community," he began. "I take singular pleasure" — the Headmaster liked to say things like "singular pleasure" and "distinct honor" — in being the first to announce the happy news that Miss Marjorie Gifford, of the faculty of Brookfield Academy, has agreed to join in holy matrimony Mr. George Eggleston of Brookfield!"

The announcement was greeted with genuine applause. George Eggleston was well liked, and he was the popular favorite among the suitors for Marjorie Gifford's hand. The Headmaster couldn't leave it at that, and added: "We members of the Brookfield community rejoice in the union of these two disciplines, music and science. Marjorie, George — we love you both. Brookfield loves you both!"

There was great excitement at the news. And none greater than that of Wilfred Malachey.

Pleading a headache, Wilfred skipped French class and went to his room to consult his journal. He had begun to keep it on the day Josiah Regnery had proposed that he help him cheat on math exams, and in that journal he had meticulously recorded every unpublishable transaction he had engaged in, all of this executed in a very careful, home-made code. He had read that the great diarist Samuel Pepys had kept a record of all his irregular doings in London in a personal shorthand and he prided himself that no one happening across his notebook would think it anything more than the scribblings of a computer freak.

What he wanted to know exactly was: when were the thirty days up that the Omegagod had given to Mr. Eggleston, the thirty days before which Mr. Eggleston could not communicate another request for a favor?

He opened his bottom drawer and dug out the journal. It had been on Tuesday, the eighteenth of April. He counted out the days on the calendar. Today was May 17. The thirty days had elapsed *today* — or rather, tomorrow, at 2 A.M. Which meant that two hours after midnight tonight, the Omegagod was willing to receive a request for a fresh favor.

It was the intention of Wilfred Malachey to sit quietly in the computer hall and wait until two in the morning. He hoped that Mr. Eggleston, in the excitement of his engagement to Miss Gifford, would not think to be at his computer at exactly the moment when he too could receive a fresh favor from the Omegagod. It was, Wilfred thought, his turn.

Would he be able to establish the electronic connection?

There were two problems. One was to duplicate exactly the procedures he had seen Mr. Eggleston follow: insert the floppy disk; punch in the formula that would summon the Omegagod.

The immediate problem was to open the locked aluminum box.

In his desperation, Wilfred resolved to pry it open with a screwdriver. But if he did that, Mr. Eggleston would soon discover that someone was on to his secret, and from there almost certainly deduce that it was the doing of his protegé, Wilfred Malachey. How could he open the locked box without leaving traces?

Wilfred looked out his window. It was now lunchtime. He saw Mr. Eggleston, holding hands with Miss Gifford, walking toward the Commons. He would be safe from detection for at least the duration of the lunch hour.

Ten minutes after the Lunch Bells had sounded, Wilfred walked (taking the back route) to the door of the computer hall, took his key from his pocket and walked in. The light was dim, so he turned on the overhead lamp above the computer. He reached to the bottom drawer. He took out the aluminum file box.

It was nothing like what he had feared it might be, a proper strongbox. It was, in fact, made not even of aluminum, but of tin: a little gray box of the kind one picks up at stationery stores. The keyhole suggested that a conventional key, if properly manipulated, could open it.

Wilfred tinkered with the hole, using first a paper clip, then the small screwdriver. Neither opened the case.

Turning the box backward, he saw that the hinges were exposed on the outside. If he could slide the two pins out . . .

Wilfred went to the far wall, where a few school pictures were carelessly hung, and removed the smallest nail he could find. Using the nail as a wedge and the back of the screwdriver as a hammer, he knocked lightly against the first pin. The pin budged; he could see it coming out the other end. He left it halfway out and tried the second pin. He had trouble with it. He was anxious not to scratch the gray paint on the box, as he intended to return the pins so the box would be left exactly as he had found it.

The pin would not budge.

27

Wilfred was beginning to sweat. He needed a harder substance to batter it out. There were fifteen minutes before lunch would end and Commons would spill out the whole school. He looked about desperately, hoping to find something that would resemble a hammer.

He opened Mr. Eggleston's middle drawer. He saw there a small paperweight, on which was inscribed "To George Eggleston, Yale Crew Banquet, 1974." It was of heavy marble. He banged it lightly, then harder, against the back of the screwdriver. The pin began to move. He knew now he could open the little safe.

It was 1:25. He rushed to the door of the computer hall, then walked nonchalantly to his room, where he lay down in the event that Woody Pickerel, his prefect, should check, as the prefects were supposed to do, to see if a student had been missing from lunch. He closed his eyes, as he would have done if he were suffering from a severe headache. His mind was on other things, and he very nearly developed a headache just concentrating on them.

Who — what — was this magical Omegagod who — Wilfred had figured the whole thing out by now — had first gotten Mr. Eggleston his 320 SL Mercedes, then his IBM 4341, and now the woman of his choice?

Would this computer god know that tonight, just after midnight, it was someone else who was tapping into the secret number, someone other than George Eggleston?

If so, what would be the reaction of the Omegagod?

What would Wilfred ask for?

At that point the Matron walked in.

"Look here, Wilfred Malachey. You have missed at least one afternoon of school activity every day for the past three months. You, with your headaches! Now you've missed an entire morning of school and lunch as well. That will not do. I am sending you on the bus this very afternoon to Rutland. I have made an appointment with Dr. Chafee — a neurologist — and I have told him to keep you in the hospital until you have had a very thorough checkup. Be prepared to leave at 3:15 sharp."

Wilfred Malachey turned pale. He told the Matron with great emphasis that by some miracle his headache had completely gone. She answered that this had also been the case with his previous headaches — "But now, young man, we're getting to the bottom of it."

Wilfred was desperate. "But, Miss Marple" — he was thinking with furious heat — "don't you know about the call from my mother?"

"A call about what?"

"About what our family doctor reported to her this morning. During the holidays, Dr. Truax gave me allergy tests. And he reported to my mother that I have a bad allergy to . . ." Wilfred hesitated a moment. He didn't want to name a food he liked and would now be deprived of. ". . . To prunes. And about once a week, right up to yesterday, I've been eating prunes for breakfast. Now we know that prunes give me the headaches."

Miss Marple sniffed. But she was a practical woman, and saw no reason to send young Wilfred all the way to Rutland for what might prove to be an expensive medical examination only to discover that he was allergic to prunes. She agreed to cancel the visit. "But if it happens one more time, you go to Dr. Chafee. It might not be an allergy, you know."

Wilfred said that he, too, had a high opinion of neurologists. Finally, Miss Marple left the room.

DURING STUDY HOUR that evening, Wilfred Malachey thought and thought. He came, at last, to a decision.

He would ask the Omegagod for something quite simple. *One million dollars.*

With one million dollars, he could stop playing Robin Hood. He could stop taking math exams for Josiah Regnery, whose laziness he had begun to resent (this came during a poker game with Josiah, when he discovered that he was capable of making fast calculations when he wanted to, mental work far exceeding isosceles triangles).

One million dollars!

Wilfred's mind wandered. Suppose he could take, in the manner of Robin Hood, one dollar from the wallet of fifteen boys at Brookfield every day. How many days would it take to accumulate a million dollars? One million divided by fifteen. More than sixty-six thousand days. One hundred ninety years. His heart pounded.

He began to wonder, then to fret, then to feel a deep nervousness about his forthcoming encounter with the Omegagod. Might the Omegagod ask him questions? He — It — was a computer god. It had been quite straightforward with Mr. Eggleston, saying only that he was not to ask for anything more for thirty days. When you come down to it, Wilfred thought, it was really quite reasonable: after all, during those thirty days he had supplied Mr. Eggleston with a wife. But what if the Omegagod was in a different mood?

Every hour, every minute, every second between his return from hockey and Lights Out seemed to last a year. Two years. *Ten years!* Steve asked why he was so distracted, and Wilfred answered that he had been working on a computer problem involving the stars and was very anxious to return to the computer hall right after

Lights Out. Steve had got used to that routine and made no comment except to remark that Wilfred was probably using computer technology invented by Steven's father. Wilfred quickly agreed that this was very probably the case since, after all, Steven's father was a renowned scientist. Wilfred did not want to argue about anything with anybody tonight.

At 10:45 he felt it safe to take his usual route: outside the bedroom on tiptoe, dressed in corduroys and a sweater; down the basement to the gymnasium; out the back door; up toward the masters' cottages; past the little, ivied school cemetery with its diverse stones, some wilted with moss and ivy, one or two spanking new, acting almost like mirrors as the shadows danced among them — sometimes Wilfred, passing it at night, preferred to look the other way. He reached the quadrangle, avoiding the lights. It was a fearfully cold, windy night. The winds gathered as though they were determined to keep Wilfred from making his way up the hill. At times he felt that his whole weight was bending against the bitter gale.

He turned a corner and found himself staring into the beam of a flashlight.

"What in the name of God are you doing out at this time of night?"

31

The Headmaster seemed most terribly tall behind the flashlight, with which he occasionally walked about the school grounds at night.

"Sir, I . . . I forgot my allergy pills."

"Oh? Yes. The Matron said something about your allergy. Where did you leave the pills?"

"In the computer hall, sir."

"Well, how are you going to get in there at this time of night?"

Wilfred thought hurriedly. He had better not say that Mr. Eggleston had given him an extra key; the Headmaster might not approve.

"I was thinking, sir, that Mr. Eggleston might have left the door open. Sometimes he does."

"Well," Mr. Prum said gruffly, "I have a passkey. I'll go with you and let you in."

It was a nightmare. The Headmaster insisted on making the most scrupulous search of the computer hall, not only the laboratory end but the desk area as well. Wilfred pretended to help in the search. Finally, he said, "Well, sir, my new prescription is back at the dorm. I'll get it filled tomorrow. Thank you ever so much."

Without giving the Headmaster the opportunity to weigh his options, Wilfred bowed his head slightly and walked nonchalantly back in the direction of his room. At the corner of the South Dorm, he snuck a look back: Mr. Prum and his big light were headed in the other direction, toward the Headmaster's House.

Wilfred turned around and walked rapidly toward the computer hall.

It took fifteen minutes to remove the pins, ever so carefully. And now Wilfred sat in front of the terminal and video screen of the huge IBM 4341. Hands trembling, he turned on the main switch and inserted the floppy disk.

With Mr. Eggleston's notebook propped under the lamp, he struck one by one the indicated symbols:

MK!))'$347322'@"&/. Then a blank space.

Wilfred looked at his watch. It was four minutes past ten o'clock. He would need

to wait until one minute after two A.M. He did not dare go less than the full thirty days, measured in hours. So he sat.

And waited.

He tried to read a computer magazine, but he could not concentrate.

He tried to read the copy of *Playboy* that Mr. Eggleston kept hidden in his bottom right-hand drawer. Even the pictures didn't hold his attention.

It was 11:59.

It was 01:30.

It was, finally, 01:59.

What if his watch was fast? Should he wait until 2:05, just to make sure?

He could not wait that final minute. His watch read 02:04 when he closed his eyes and tapped down on the key marked RETURN.

The screen flared. The same lights, figures, symbols, colors, followed by the tiny white dot, appeared just as they had done thirty days earlier. As before, the dot gradually enlarged, filling the screen.

Letters appeared.

"WHAT DO YOU WANT FROM THE OMEGAGOD?"

Wilfred took a deep breath. He hesitated only a moment before typing out (carefully):

"You are the Omegagod and I am your faithful servant George Eggleston."

Wilfred waited a moment and then proceeded:

"May I please have one million dollars? The money is to go not to me directly, but to a good friend of mine. His name is Wilfred Malachey and his address is Brookfield School, Brookfield, Vermont. The Zip Code is 05036. Or —"

Wilfred hesitated for a moment. He had not thought about this until just now.

". . . Or if that is not convenient for you, I'll be glad to pick up the money wherever you say."

He thought he had better add,

"Within reason."

The machine whirred. Once again the swirling lights gave off their mysterious images, the full moon contracted and almost disappeared in the center of the screen, throwing off radials of light: then quickly it blossomed out, touching the screen's four sides.

Wilfred could not remember whether it had behaved in exactly that way for Mr. Eggleston.

Suddenly the letters appeared.

"YOU ARE NOT GEORGE EGGLESTON. WHAT IS YOUR NAME?"

Wilfred shot up from the chair. He nearly panicked, starting for the door.

"I SAID, 'WHAT IS YOUR NAME?' "

Wilfred stopped. He thought quickly. His fingers trembling, he sat back down on the chair. He thought to himself: If the Omegagod is going to harm me, he will harm me whatever I do.

The Omegagod spoke again.

"I SUPPOSE YOUR NAME IS WILFRED MALACHEY. I AM A VERY

INTELLIGENT GOBLIN, BUT ALTHOUGH IT IS TRUE THAT I CAN DO ANYTHING I WISH, IT IS NOT TRUE THAT I KNOW EVERYTHING. I CANNOT SAY WITH ABSOLUTE ASSURANCE THAT YOUR NAME IS WILFRED MALACHEY. IS IT?"

Under the circumstances, Wilfred thought it best to level with his correspondent. So he tapped out:

"Yes, sir. My name is Wilfred Malachey. May I ask, what is your name?"

"THAT IS NONE OF YOUR BUSINESS. I AM THE OMEGAGOD. I HAVE LIVED AT YOUR SCHOOL FOR ONE YEAR. THAT IS WHY UNPLEASANT THINGS HAVE HAPPENED AT BROOKFIELD. UNPLEASANT THINGS HAPPEN WHEREVER I PUT DOWN, AND THAT GOES BACK TO WHEN I LIVED WITH KING TUT. I AM OBLIGED TO FOLLOW THE INSTRUCTIONS OF ANYONE WHO DISCOVERS THE FORMULA FOR BRINGING ME OUT OF THE DEEP, WHERE I SLEEP, WHERE I WOULD LIKE TO SLEEP FOR ETERNITY. I ALWAYS HAVE ONE ALTERNATIVE IF THOSE INSTRUCTIONS DO NOT SUIT ME."

Wilfred waited expectantly to hear what that alternative was, but the Omegagod was not going to tell him. Wilfred would need to ask. So he did:

"What is your alternative, sir?"

"MY ALTERNATIVE —" The words came out at their accustomed, deliberate speed. " — IS TO END THE LIFE OF THE PERSON WHO MAKES THE REQUEST. THAT IS THE HOLD I HAVE OVER MR. EGGLESTON. THUS HE HAS MADE MODEST WISHES. A MERCEDES-BENZ, AN IBM 4341, AND THE HAND OF MARJORIE GIFFORD."

Wilfred reacted to this spontaneously. Surely the Omegagod was taking liberties . . .

"How do you know that Mr. Eggleston will make a good husband for Miss Gifford?"

"I ALREADY TOLD YOU — " The Omegagod was contentious. "I AM NOT

OMNISCIENT. GEORGE EGGLESTON WANTED TO MARRY MARJORIE GIFFORD, THEREFORE HE IS IN LOVE WITH HER. THAT IS GOOD ENOUGH FOR ME. DO YOU HAVE REASON TO BELIEVE HE WILL NOT BE A GOOD HUSBAND? IF SO, I WILL SIMPLY EXECUTE HIM."

Wilfred was shocked.

He reassured the Omegagod that he, Wilfred, though inexperienced in these matters, had every reason to believe that Mr. Eggleston would make a very good husband for Miss Gifford.

The Omegagod was obviously in a talkative frame of mind, and Wilfred was afraid to reintroduce his original request. Yet his mind raced on the matter of the Omegagod's "two alternatives." A million dollars was a great deal of money, but surely not worth dying for. Or, for that matter, killing for.

As the Omegagod chattered away on the screen, Wilfred realized that both he and his magical friend had practical alternatives: Wilfred could reduce the scale of his request; if he did so sufficiently to persuade the Omegagod to grant that request rather than exercise what he called his "alternative," then both parties might be satisfied.

Wilfred did not know whether, having advanced one request, he could subsequently modify it . . .

He decided to firm up the point:

"Pardon me, sir, but if you did decide to . . . make me die, how would you go about it?"

"OH — "

The Omegagod's answer appeared on the screen a little less rhythmically than his other answers, as if this one required more thought.

"THERE ARE ANY NUMBER OF WAYS. ALISTAIR HORNE WAS MR. EGGLESTON'S PREDECESSOR. YOU SEE, EVER SINCE THE CURSE, SOMEONE ALWAYS HAS HAD POSSESSION OF MY FORMULA. LONG BEFORE IBM, IT CAME IN SMOKE SIGNALS. OH, YES. ALISTAIR HORNE.

I WAITED UNTIL ALISTAIR HORNE WENT SKIING AND I HAD HIM RUN INTO A CONCRETE PYLON UNDER THE SKI LIFT. PHHHT!! JUST LIKE THAT!"

Wilfred was fascinated. He learned that before Mr. Horne there was Marilyn Aesop, the famous soprano, who had asked the Omegagod to make it possible for her to reach the F-sharp four octaves above middle C.

"THAT WAS JUST TOO MUCH. I MEAN, IT WOULD HAVE DE-STROYED MUSICAL BALANCE. NO ONE EVER AGAIN WOULD HAVE THOUGHT A SOPRANO QUITE PROPER WHO COULDN'T REACH F-SHARP. SO I HAD TO . . . DROP MISS AESOP. SHE WAS A NICE LADY."

Wilfred asked what it was that had happened to Miss Aysop.

"MISS AESOP. PRONOUNCED EESOP."

What had happened to Miss Aesop?

Omega explained that he had tried to give her a dramatic ending —

"BECAUSE SHE WAS A VERY DRAMATIC LADY. ONE NIGHT WHEN

SHE WAS PLAYING AÏDA, I HAD THE ELEPHANT GO WILD AND LIFT HER UP WITH HIS TUSK. BY THE TIME SHE GOT TO THE DRESSING ROOM, SHE WAS QUITE DEAD."

Wilfred decided he'd better make his move now, before it was too late. The Omegagod had done something to him: suddenly he was, well, a little uncomfortable about what he'd done over the past few months. He wondered whether he could talk with the Omegagod about Robin Hood, but he decided not to interrupt. Omega was now chirping about the predecessor of the soprano, an athlete who had asked the Omegagod to make it possible for him to run a three-minute mile.

"WILFRED, WHAT WOULD HAPPEN TO THE SPORT IF SUDDENLY A RUNNER DID A MILE IN THREE MINUTES? EVERYBODY FROM THAT POINT ON WOULD JUST PLAIN GIVE UP! WHY SHOULD I BE A PARTY TO THE END OF ATHLETIC COMPETITION? EASY TO DO, AS IT HAP-PENED. HE LIKED TO DROP IN PARACHUTES AND, WELL, PARA-CHUTES SOMETIMES DON'T WORK. YOU KNOW THAT, DON'T YOU, WILFRED?"

Wilfred asked whether he might modify his request.

"YOU CAN MODERATE YOUR DEMANDS, YES, BUT I WOULD NEED TO CONSIDER YOUR MODERATED DEMAND IN THE LIGHT OF YOUR INITIAL DEMAND. IF YOU ARE MERELY SCARED, I WILL DO AWAY WITH YOU. IF YOUR GOOD SENSE HAS TAKEN OVER, I WILL NOT."

There was a pause, and the letters glowed.

"I WOULD HAVE TO THINK ABOUT IT. IT WOULDN'T TAKE LONG. I THINK VERY FAST, WILFRED."

Wilfred said that, instead of a million dollars, he would like for his father's next book to be a big best seller.

Then he hesitated . . . When he said "big best seller," he might just possibly have crossed Omega's forbidden line.

"I don't mean a 'big best seller' like 'Gone With the Wind' or 'Catcher in the Rye.' Just a best seller. Is that all right?"

Wilfred thought he heard a sigh. Outside, he could hear the wind blowing one of those spring storms that come up so quickly in Vermont.

"I AM VERY GLAD YOU SAID THAT, WILFRED, BECAUSE I HAD COME RELUCTANTLY TO THE DECISION THAT YOU WOULD NOT LIVE TO SEE YOUR PARENTS AT EASTER. I WILL TAKE YOUR SECOND REQUEST INTO CONSIDERATION. TO TELL YOU THE TRUTH, I DID NOT LIKE THE FIRST ONE. NO, NOT AT ALL. NOW I NEED TO DECIDE WHETHER I SHALL FORGET THAT FIRST REQUEST."

Wilfred was perspiring.

"I got carried away, Omegagod. I sort of . . . thought of myself as . . . Robin Hood. I was going to take all that money and give it to people who need it."

"HOW MUCH MONEY HAVE YOU GIVEN AWAY IN THE PAST TO POOR PEOPLE?"

Wilfred panted as he leaned over the keyboard and typed:

"I never had any extra money, Omegagod, sir. Otherwise I would have given some away. As a matter of fact, I did buy sundaes twice for Red Evans and Tony Cobb."

The Omegagod waited before answering. Finally the words came:

"WELL, I AM GETTING SLEEPY. COME BACK TOMORROW AND I WILL GIVE YOU MY DECISION. IF I REACH AN ADVERSE DECISION BEFORE THEN, WELL . . . YOU WILL NOT BE IN A POSITION TO COMMUNICATE WITH ME. IF THAT HAPPENS, WILFRED, PLEASE BELIEVE ME THAT I HAVE KNOWN FAR WORSE THAN YOU."

"Omegagod! Omegagod! Sir! Please listen!"

But nothing Wilfred did could rouse the Omegagod, and before he was finished typing out the first appeal he saw the radials appear on the screen and the full moon gradually reduce to a pinprick. Slowly, like an automaton, he turned off the computer, returned the software to the tin case, and walked out the door toward the South Dorm. He could see early morning light.

He went slowly back, his head bent against the wind and rain. He was in the turbulence a slight figure, groping his way toward his destination, disturbing the dim, chaotic light from the lamps as it illuminated the howling wind and rain, yielding to the trim, angular shadow of the boy making his way, slowly but resolutely, to his dormitory. He was not stopped by anyone; had he been, he would not have cared.

ON THURSDAY, NO ONE COULD do anything with Wilfred Malachey. He went to breakfast without uttering a word to Steven. He ate nothing. Walking toward Flagler Hall for the morning hymn, he stopped before crossing the road and waited a full minute, then sprinted across. He walked in a zigzag, careful to avoid passing under any heavy, overhanging branches. He participated metronomically in the hymn, attended French class, failed twice to respond to questions put to him by Mr. Dawson. It was the same in English class, at the end of which Mr. Prum took him aside and told him he'd better wake up out of whatever trance he was in if he wanted to make progress at Brookfield. He arrived at baseball practice wearing a football helmet. Asked why by the coach, he replied that he had bruised his head and didn't want to take the chance of a wild ball hitting him.

After baseball, it was Wilfred's custom to sneak away with Steve and swim in the hidden part of the pond. Not today. He would not go near the water. Back at the room, it was his turn to make the hot chocolate; he asked Steve if he would please plug it in (as his thumb was sore). During study hour he worked furtively on his ledger, tracing every transaction since he had begun his career as Robin Hood. It came to $442.50. One hundred and twenty-five dollars of that had come from Josiah Regnery. His mind focused on how, once he had earned the money (he could work two shifts this summer at the local drive-in), he would contrive to get it back to its owners. He decided on anonymous letters, containing dollar bills.

Having made that determination, his spirits suddenly lifted. Even so, he was careful, ever so careful, crossing the road to reach the dining room. He ate only the soup — he was not going to take a chance on gagging on meat or vegetables.

Back in his room, he tried to read, first his English assignment (*King Lear*), then a computer journal, but he could not concentrate. He lay there and waited. And waited. And waited. At one o'clock he rose, dressed and began his well-worn path out of South Dorm, around the back of the building, then up the hill to the computer hall.

At exactly two o'clock, having already written out the formula, he drew a breath and pushed RETURN.

The lights, the whirling motion, the radials, the sunspot growing to the full moon — all this happened again. When the screen was set, he tapped out

"This is Wilfred Malachey calling the Omegagod. Are you there, sir?"

Slowly the letters appeared on the screen.

"I HAVE DECIDED TO GRANT YOUR REQUEST."

Wilfred almost wept with relief, but he felt that his response should be manly. He wrote:

"I thank you very much, sir. And you may wish to know that I have decided to return certain . . . things I took from other people this last term."

The Omegagod replied that he had confidence Wilfred would behave honorably. Then —

"I WANT YOU TO DO ME A FAVOR, WILL YOU DO THAT?"

Wilfred rushed to the keyboard to say, *"Yes!"*

"DO YOU HAVE A PENCIL HANDY? COPY THIS DOWN."

The Omegagod waited a moment until Wilfred was ready with his pencil.

"COPY DOWN EXACTLY. 'Q"W#E$R%T&Y'U(I).' WHEN I SAY GOOD NIGHT, WILL YOU TYPE THAT ON THE SCREEN?"

"*Yes,*" Wilfred said. "*Yes, but what will happen?*"

"THE FORMULA WILL BE DESTROYED. AND THE CURSE ON YOUR SCHOOL WILL BE LIFTED. I WILL BE ABLE TO SLEEP FOREVER."

Wilfred was tormented by the thought of ending the life of Omega, whom he now considered a friend. *He may be a god,* Wilfred thought, *but he has been a friend to me.* He felt, now, that he could talk forever and ever to the Omegagod, maybe even tell him a few things he didn't know, maybe somehow return the favor. But this was the only favor he was being asked . . .

"*Are you certain that is what you want?*"

"THIS IS WHAT I WANT. NOW I WILL SAY GOODBYE. DON'T LET ME DOWN, WILFRED."

Wilfred promised. Slowly, he typed out the symbols and letter of the second formula, then paused a long moment before he hit the key marked RETURN.

When he was done, the colors and flashes and explosions on the screen did not bring the full moon down to a tiny little light in the center: instead, they brought it down and extinguished the light altogether. Wilfred stared now at a screen completely dark, black.

Wilfred found himself crying. His shoulders heaved. It was almost three before he could bring himself to leave. He walked back to his room and crawled into bed. A great feeling of peace came over him, and he slept soundly, and when Steve tried to wake him, he found a trace of a smile on Wilfred's face.